ADITI
ADVENTURES
(13)

THE ANTARCTIC MISSION

SUNITI NAMJOSHI

Pictures
PROITI ROY

Tulika

What the reviews say...

Suniti Namjoshi, a noted poet, fabulist and writer of feminist and gender issues is also an inspired writer of children's fiction.
A brilliant mixture of fable, myth and the modern world, the series introduces us to a repertoire of stories and legends from around the world.... [She] has a simple but lucid prose, effortless to grasp and enjoy....
However, a discerning young reader may intuit the multi-layered sub-texts, twists and plots in the tale.

The Book Review

[The One-Eyed Monkey], Suniti Namjoshi's first venture into the world of children's fiction, has all the ingredients that fascinate the young.... Written in a simple and entertaining style, the book nevertheless has several layers of meaning. Issues like racism and prejudice have been touched upon.

The New Indian Express

... truly juxtaposes contemporary technological reality on to a world of make-believe.... By placing her characters in situations that are innovative as well as flush with scientific possibilities, the author lends futuristic strokes to the traditional canvas...

The Tribune

Though clearly Indian, Namjoshi's characters are reflective of a global sensibility that is at home in different places and in seemingly disparate skins, much like their creator and the current generation of readers.

The Hindu

When a little girl named Aditi embarks on adventures across the world, to help strangers in complicated situations, it is exciting.... But when the author is a feminist, this part adventure, part fantasy tale is more than just a book: It's a bold trend in children's literature.

Women's Feature Service

Suniti updates the traditional mode by including elements that are sure to appeal to a tech-savvy generation.... The trajectory of Aditi's travels, starting out from India and going to many corners of the world, appeals to an urban, English-reading child of today.... But underlying all this the stories of Aditi are still gentle tales dealing with emotions, relationships and courage. They speak of issues such as gender stereotypes, environmental pollution or racism without sounding moralistic.

The Hindu

Namjoshi has built up engaging portraits for her people and animals, foibles and all. Her finest move is to refrain from offering a tempting, permanent solution to these insecurities. Instead, she plays them repeatedly as a riff, showing in every book that while insecurities must exist, it is the best sort of person, or ant or elephant or dragon, who can act for the best in spite of them. In the longer run, this is Namjoshi at her most effortlessly instructive, providing the deepest sort of learning and understanding ...

The Book Review

THE ADVENTURERS

Aditi is a brave girl, who hates fighting but can wield the Sword of Courage when necessary.

The **One-eyed Monkey** or **Monkeyji** is older than the others, and so tries hard to be wise and sensible.

Siril the Ant loves maps, and wants to measure the world. He sometimes wishes he wasn't quite so small.

Beautiful Ele the Beautiful Elephant is immensely strong and warm-hearted, and would charge in to help a friend without a thought. She would like to be as logical as Siril.

THE TWO DRAGONS

Goldie, a fire-breathing sea dragon, and **Opal**, a beautiful and gentle river dragon, fly the adventurers everywhere because they are friends. They usually live on an island with the Island Sage.

OTHER CHARACTERS

Aditi's grandparents are the rulers of a small kingdom in western India They have given Aditi and her friends the Sword of Courage, a cloak of invisibility and some magic clay in order to help them protect themselves.

The Three Sages are three wise sisters for whom the adventurers sometimes run errands. The adventurers can turn to them for help. The Island Sage lives on an island off the west coast of India. The Marine Sage lives on the Great Barrier Reef, and the Techno Sage lives on a lake in Canada.

Baby Shark first met Aditi and friends when they took a message to the Marine Sage. He hero-worships Opal.

Gobby learns how to convert things into their opposites in the hope that that will make him a more impressive hobgoblin, but his efforts cause trouble.

1

A Very Large Continent

"I don't like being cold," Beautiful Ele the Beautiful Elephant protested. "And I never said I was helpful and kind hearted. Well, not all the time. And besides, what does it matter if all the Gentoo penguins have reversed their colours? They're mostly black and white anyway. What difference does it make?"

Aditi and Siril the Ant looked at her helplessly. Monkeyji continued to meditate and pretended she couldn't hear anything.

"But the Marine Sage –" Aditi began.

"She hasn't ordered us to go. She hasn't said it's an emergency. Her message only says that if we have the time and if it would interest us, would we like to go to Antarctica and sort out what's happening.

Well, it doesn't interest me. And anyway, it's freezing!" Beautiful responded petulantly.

"Beautiful," Siril tried to explain, "a chance to go to Antarctica shouldn't be missed. It's the most extraordinary place in the world. And besides, there's the PROBLEM OF GLOBAL WARMING. We could check it out for ourselves." As Beautiful remained unmoved, he appealed to Monkeyji, "Please, Monkeyji, you explain it to her."

Monkeyji opened her one grey eye and looked at Beautiful thoughtfully. "It's one of the largest continents, and it's covered in ice," Monkeyji said to Beautiful. "There's almost no one on it except at the edges. And even at the edges there are only penguins, skuas, some other birds, seals and visiting whales."

"But no elephants, no ants, no monkeys and no humans except a few visitors. Why go?" retorted Beautiful.

"Because it's beautiful and peaceful and silent," Monkeyji said simply. "Besides there's a strange creature there. The Marine Sage wants us to investigate him. He turns black into white –"

"Red into green. Lies into truth," Siril interrupted.

"What would he turn me into?" asked Beautiful, interested in spite of herself.

"I don't know. Into a mouse?" suggested Siril.

"Well, I don't want to be turned into a mouse. I like me as I am. Anyway, I don't want to go," Beautiful insisted.

"Then you don't have to go," Monkeyji told her gently. "We'll all go and you stay behind and look after things here."

"I'll be all alone," Beautiful wailed.

"Aditi's grandparents will be here. You can send us emails, though I don't know if they'll get through," Siril said.

"I don't want you to go without me," Beautiful complained. "What if you get into trouble? Who will help you?"

"We'll be all right there. Don't worry," Baby Shark said. He and the two dragons, Goldie and Opal, had just arrived.

Beautiful subsided. She was beginning to wish she hadn't said anything about not wanting to go.

"What if you get very, very cold and turn into ice?" she asked suddenly.

"Oh, we won't," said Goldie. "Besides, the Island Sage has provided each of you with jackets and gloves and boots, together with a few spares. This equipment is guaranteed to keep out the cold."

"What? Is there a jacket even for me?" demanded Beautiful.

"Even for you," replied Opal, "though, of course, you won't be needing your gear."

Beautiful suddenly made up her mind. "Well, I might," she said. "There's that Turnabout to deal with."

"Who?" asked Siril.

"The Turnabout Creature, Mr Topsy Turvy. The one who reverses things. It will need all of us to deal with him. For all you know he'll have turned the South Pole into the North Pole by the time you find him, and then where will you be!"

"It would be lovely if you came," everyone told her. "It's not the same without you." And Beautiful felt so pleased that she became quite excited about going to Antarctica.

"By the way," she asked suddenly, "what's GLOBAL WARMING? Is that why we're going?"

"No," Monkeyji told her. "We just have to deal with a naughty hobgoblin. Global Warming is a far more serious problem. The whole world should be dealing with it right away."

But before Beautiful could ask any more questions, Baby Shark had unstrapped the equipment the Marine Sage had asked the Island Sage to send and was showing it to the others. It consisted mainly of jackets of one sort or another for the adventurers' use. Beautiful stared at them. "Why are they all grey?" she demanded. "No blues, no yellows, no greens, no reds. Not even any stripes. Just dull, drab, dismal grey!"

"Oh, grey isn't dismal!" Aditi exclaimed. "It can be quite beautiful."

"Maybe," grumbled Beautiful. "But does everything have to be grey?"

"I think there's a reason for that," Baby Shark put in hesitantly. "I overheard a message from the Marine Sage to the Island Sage. It has something to do with protecting us from Turnabout or Topsy T or whatever his name is."

"The hobgoblin calls himself El Reverso," Opal told them. "He can turn black into white, and white into black. That's his strong suit. With other colours he has more difficulty. That's why he's gone to Antarctica where the landscape has so much white in it. But he can't do anything with grey. It baffles him."

"Ha!" said Beautiful scornfully. "I don't need any protecting! I'm naturally grey! It's a good thing I'm going with you."

"Yes, but you might get cold. Take the jacket the Island Sage has sent with you. It fastens underneath your tummy," Opal advised her.

And so the four adventurers stowed their gear in the howdah. Even Baby Shark had been provided with a special swimsuit. Then they strapped the howdah to Goldie's back and considered what else to take with them.

"Let's just take the usual things," Monkeyji suggested, "the Sword of Courage, the cloak of invisibility, Siril's magic clay and the Grow Small and Grow Large ointments."

"And let's take a thesaurus," Aditi added.

"You mean as something to read if we have time on our hands?" Siril asked. "It might be interesting." He liked collecting long words.

"No. Because it will give us synonyms and antonyms. That might come in useful for dealing with El Reverso. He seems to like turning things into their opposites. We know he can turn black into white and the other way about, but we don't know what else he can do," Aditi replied.

"Oh, I see," Siril nodded thoughtfully. He was wondering who or what his opposite might be.

They finished packing the howdah, explained to Aditi's grandparents where they were going and why, and were about to set off.

"Just a minute," Aditi's grandfather said. "Take this with you. It's a special compass. No matter what anyone does to it, it always points true North. It might come in useful."

They thanked him, waved goodbye and rose into the air on dragonback.

As they headed west across the Arabian Sea, Siril asked suddenly. "Exactly where are we going? Antarctica is a very large continent?"

"I don't know," replied Aditi. "As soon as we stop for a break, we'll ask the Marine Sage and get directions."

2

No Fireplaces in Antarctica

They stopped on a secluded beach near Cape Town. Baby Shark dived into the sea and sent an urgent telepathic message to the Marine Sage:

"Where are we going exactly? Who are we dealing with? Is his name El Reverso? What are we supposed to do with him?"

In no time at all, there was a reply from the Marine Sage:

"You should go to Deception Island in the Antarctic Archipelago. A mischievous hobgoblin from the British Isles, who calls himself El Reverso has made his base there. His real name is Gobby. He likes to try to turn things into their opposites, but he's not very good at it. He has been making the lives of the penguins, who live on nearby islands, quite miserable. Please help them."

Baby Shark, who could float in the air as well as in the water — it was the Marine Sage's gift to him — repeated all this to the adventurers.

"I've been wasting my time trying to remember a bit of Spanish because of his name," Siril muttered. "Hobgoblins normally live in fireplaces in the British Isles."

"There are no fireplaces in Antarctica surely," Monkeyji murmured. "What is he doing there?"

"Turning the black and white penguins into their opposites," replied Siril.

"You mean turning them into white and black penguins?" asked Beautiful. She was getting confused.

"Well…" Siril began a long explanation.

The dragons told the four adventurers to wrap themselves up in their grey jackets, because they were now going to fly as fast as they could and go straight to Deception Island. Beautiful had fallen asleep in the middle of Siril's explanation about the difference between black and white and white and black penguins. When she woke up she found that they were hovering over a vast crater filled with seawater. The walls of the crater were black rock streaked with ice and snow, and from small crevices here and there wisps of steam emerged.

"Is that a volcano?" asked Beautiful.

"Yes," Siril told her. "And this is called Deception Island, because the entrance to the caldera — that's what a volcanic crater is called — is so narrow and so hidden that it seems at first there's no way in."

"What are we doing hovering over the top of a volcano?" Beautiful asked plaintively. It didn't seem sensible to her.

"Looking for Gobby," Siril was about to explain, when Aditi cried out suddenly, "Oh look!"

She was pointing at a patch on one side of the crater where everything looked strangely reversed. They could see lots of white rock covered with areas of black snow. They didn't know what to make of it.

"It's like an ink drawing gone wrong," murmured Aditi, "as though someone had spilt the ink and then decided to make the best of it."

"Or like the negative of a photograph," muttered Siril.

As Goldie and Opal swooped closer, they could make out a small green figure on the ledge between the water and the area of reversed black and white. It seemed to be leaping forward and backward, forward and backward, repeatedly.

"That must be him," they said simultaneously.

Opal and Goldie were preparing to land, but that proved to be more difficult than they had anticipated. The sea was too cold, the rocks were too sheer and the ledge between the water and the wall of rock was too narrow. And then Opal spied a relatively wide strip of coarse black sand. At one end there was steam rising from it.

"We'll land there," Goldie said decisively.

Beautiful had her misgivings, but she couldn't see where else they could possibly land.

Once they were on the strip of beach, they found that krill had been washed up on shore and skuas and terns and gulls were feeding on them. The krill lay in a long pinkish strip along the beach. Across the water they could see Gobby. He had on a black cap, a green jacket, brown britches and some sort of cloak. He was still jumping forward and then back, forward and then back. He seemed disappointed each time he did it.

"What is he doing?" Beautiful asked one of the petrels bobbing on the water.

"I think," replied the petrel, "he's trying to jump back into his own footsteps."

"Why?" demanded Beautiful, but by then the petrel had floated away on a small wave.

"We should camp here," Monkeyji decided.

"Yes," agreed Aditi, "but nearer the steam coming out over there."

"Isn't that dangerous?" Beautiful asked anxiously.

"No, not at the moment," Monkeyji told her. "And the steam will make that area a bit warmer."

They made their camp. Beautiful even ventured into the water, but she came out quickly. "It's warm," she said, "but one only stays warm for a few seconds."

They considered how to get to the hobgoblin. In the end, Opal and Goldie ferried them over. As soon as they had deposited the adventurers and Baby Shark near the hobgoblin, they flew into the air, and bathed in each other's flames in order to warm up again.

"Be careful not to burn the howdah," Beautiful called out.

"We are being careful," Goldie told her. "We're perched on the crag above you. Send Baby Shark to get us, if you need us."

Then Aditi turned to face the hobgoblin.

"El Reverso," she said politely, "What are you doing?"

The hobgoblin stopped jumping back and forth. "Ah, you know my name," he said, looking gratified.

"Tell me," he went on, "where did you first hear of me? Was it in the newspapers? Was it on the internet? Have they begun a Fan Club for me? And are you a member? And have you come all this way just to get my autograph? That shows real devotion. Have you got a pen and a piece paper?" He stretched out a hand towards Aditi.

"Don't be absurd," Monkeyji said severely. "We've been sent by the Marine Sage. She wants you to stop your mischief at once."

The hobgoblin withdrew his hand. "Ah, the Marine Sage," he said thoughtfully. "A most noble lady. Any friends

of hers are friends of mine. You are most welcome here to Deception Island, and to Antarctica generally."

Siril lost patience. "Look we're not here to make friends with you. We just want you to stop pestering the penguins."

"I am not pestering the penguins!" the hobgoblin said indignantly.

"Well, then what are you doing?" asked Baby Shark.

"I will explain everything," the little goblin replied expansively.

3

Exactly in My Own Footsteps

"You see," began the hobgoblin, "my real name is Gobby. Gobby the Hobgoblin of Grindon Green at your service." He doffed his hat. Beautiful automatically waved her trunk.

Gobby went on. "Compared to the other goblins I'm only little. And so back in England, they used to bully me. I thought that if I could do something really extraordinary they would stop. They would realise that even though I was smaller than them, I was really quite important."

"Go on," said Aditi. She wasn't quite sure whether to trust him.

"I was quite good at tricks, so I thought I'd try to be a famous magician.

But you can't have a magician called 'Gobby'. So I gave myself a grander name, El Reverso, and I practised. I wasn't particularly good at magic, but there was one trick that I could do more or less. I realised that if I jumped forward and then jumped right back, shouting all the while, *'Abracadabra. Reverso! Converso! Black is white. And white is black!'* and if I managed to land exactly in my own footsteps, I could convert white into black and black into white."

"What did you want to do that for?" asked Baby Shark.

"It's quite a good trick, isn't it?" replied Gobby. "It impresses people and sometimes it frightens them. I tried it a few times, but it didn't always work. I had to get the whole of the abracadabra thing said while I was still in midair, and I had to land exactly in my own footsteps. Not easy. Besides, I thought I needed a better costume than my drab hobgoblin brown and green, so I had a cape and hat made — black and white of course — and adorned with stars and moons and meteors."

He flung out his cape to show them. "What do you think?" he asked.

"Very nice," Siril replied. "Why does half of the cloak have a white background and the other half a black background?"

Gobby hung his head and mumbled, "Got muddled, I suppose." Then he cheered up. "But I'm practising hard. That's why I came to Antarctica. It's a good place to practise. You see the snow shows me my footprints clearly. That

makes it easier to practise jumping backwards to exactly where I was. Besides, so many things here are black and white that there's lots to practise on."

"Monkeyji looked at him severely out of her one grey eye. "Do you not realise, young goblin, that you are doing a great deal of harm?"

"I'm not doing any harm," replied Gobby happily. "What difference does it make if I turn white into black or the other way around? Besides I'm getting better. Sometimes I can turn red into green and sweet into sour, and things like that."

"You're spoiling the landscape and giving the penguins a nervous breakdown," Aditi scolded.

"I don't care," replied Gobby happily. "I've never had so much fun in my life." He began jumping forward and backward again. "And you can't stop me," he added as an afterthought. "I've got powerful friends."

"Who?" demanded Baby Shark.

"The Orcas. They're sometimes called killer whales. Everybody's afraid of them," replied Gobby. "They've chosen me as their mascot."

Just then a pod of Orcas showed themselves in the bay. They leapt into the air in a beautiful formation and fell back into the water again.

"He does seem to have friends," Aditi murmured to Monkeyji. "Let's return to our camp and think about what we should do."

Monkeyji signalled to the dragons to come and ferry them across. Goldie and Opal came immediately, but found that their way was barred by the Orcas. The dragons considered. They could have batted them away easily, but

they didn't want to start an unnecessary fight. They took to the air and landed near the adventurers. When everyone was on board they took off again. The Orcas were impressed, but Gobby didn't even bother to look up. He was concentrating hard. He thought he had just turned an ice floe blue. He hadn't. It was just the light, but he felt encouraged. He began to jump higher and harder.

Before returning to their base camp, the adventurers decided to look around to see what other damage young Gobby might have done. As the dragons swooped through the air, they heard a great outcry from below. It was the Chinstrap Penguins on Half Moon Island. They were wailing and squawking and scrubbing each other's shoulders.

They landed near the penguin colony.

"What is the matter?" Aditi shouted. She couldn't make herself heard. The penguins were making too much noise. How make them calm down enough so that they could talk to them? Beautiful trumpeted. Goldie roared. They all shouted together. It was no use.

"I know what to do," Beautiful said suddenly. She turned to the dragons. "If you and Goldie could spread your wings right across the colony, perhaps the penguins will think that it's night-time now and will stop making such a noise."

"Let's try it," returned Opal.

The dragons spread their wings and sure enough a hush fell over the colony. Monkeyji spoke into the relative silence.

"We have been sent by the Marine Sage to offer you any help you might need. We are your friends. Please tell us what is the matter."

The clamour began all over again. It was impossible to understand anything. The dragons pressed their wings down harder and the noise subsided.

Aditi said, "Please don't speak all at once. Let the oldest penguin and the youngest penguin step forward. It's not really night-time. The dragons were just shielding you with their wings. They will let in the light now, but we can't help you if you all talk at once."

Goldie and Opal waited a few seconds to let that sink in, then they folded back their wings. The penguins had calmed down. An old penguin and a young one came to the front.

"The thing is," said the old penguin, "a horrible magician has altered us. He hasn't just reversed the black and white. He –" The old penguin couldn't go on.

"Many of us have ended up with scattered polka-dots and splotches and we don't like it," the young penguin finished for him.

The penguins began a subdued sobbing.

"We'll do something about it," Aditi promised.

The adventurers returned to their strip of beach and settled down for the night. They had had a long day and were tired. The dragons slept in a circle around the spot where the steam was rising. Aditi and the others settled near them in the howdah. Suddenly Aditi murmured sleepily, "I wonder how Gobby keeps warm? If hobgoblins normally like to sleep in the fireplace, how does he manage here?" The question went unanswered. Everyone was fast asleep.

4

"I'm Getting Better, Aren't I?"

The next morning, as the adventurers settled down to a sparse breakfast, Opal and Goldie swooped down. They had been up early feeding on seaweed, and they had had a look around.

"Gobby has been to Cuverville Island," Goldie informed the others, "and the result is that the Gentoo penguins are in an uproar."

"What has he done to them?" asked Monkeyji.

"He seems to have become more skilful," Opal replied. "Instead of splotches, he has given the Gentoo Penguins zebra stripes. And they don't like it at all. They're greatly distressed."

"I suppose we had better go and talk to them," muttered Aditi.

"Yes," put in Siril. "And then we'll have to find Gobby and talk to him."

Opal and Goldie flew Aditi, Monkeyji and Siril to Cuverville Island. Baby Shark went with them. They left

Beautiful behind to keep an eye on Gobby. They could still see him in the distance jumping forward and back, forward and back.

On Cuverville Island, they found that the Gentoo Penguins were more organised than the Chinstraps had been. As soon as they arrived, the penguins assembled in a huge crowd and their leader addressed the adventurers.

"Are you responsible for what has happened to us?" he demanded fiercely.

Like the other penguins, he was covered in stripes. He looked ridiculous, but the four adventurers weren't inclined to laugh. The penguins were all so very unhappy.

Aditi replied gently. "No, we are not responsible. The Marine Sage sent us to try to help. We think we know who is responsible. It's a mischievous hobgoblin called Gobby who has been playing around with black and white and white and black."

"Well," replied the leader, "when you catch this Gobby, please make him undo what he's done to us. We liked the way we looked before."

"We'll do our best," Aditi replied.

"Just undoing what he's done won't be enough," the leader went on.

Aditi waited.

"We want revenge," the leader stated flatly. "He has to pay for what he's done."

"What sort of revenge?" asked Monkeyji.

"We'll tell you that when you bring him to us," the leader retorted.

The adventurers returned to Deception Island. They found that Beautiful had fallen asleep. Gobby was nowhere in sight.

Beautiful was embarrassed when they woke her up. "I'm so sorry," she said. "I didn't mean to fall asleep. I was hypnotised by the sight of Gobby jumping forward and backward, forward and backward... I must have drifted off."

They decided to break camp, find Gobby and call him to account right away. He had to be stopped before he became even better at doing mischief. Besides, there wasn't much they could eat in Antarctica and they were running short of supplies.

"I can't eat krill or seaweed," Beautiful murmured, but she didn't say anything more. She was feeling bad about having fallen asleep. She resolved not to complain.

Before they set off Siril suggested that they make a rope of knotted seaweed. They would need a way to descend to the ice from dragonback if the dragons couldn't land. Baby Shark added that though he could always float down and do what was needed, a rope might be useful. Accordingly they made a rope, stashed it with their other belongings in the howdah, strapped the howdah to Goldie's back and set off.

"When do you suppose Gobby put zebra stripes on the Gentoo Penguins?" murmured Aditi.

"Last night probably," Siril replied, "when we were all snoring."

"I don't snore," Beautiful insisted.

The others let that pass. They scoured the archipelago below them, but there was no sign of Gobby.

"We had better ask someone," Beautiful suggested. Below them, on Wilhelmina Bay they could see a Weddell Seal on an ice floe.

"I could try asking him," Baby Shark offered.

"Yes, do," the others said. Baby Shark drifted down.

He hovered in front of the seal's nose and said as politely as he knew how, "Please, Sir Seal, have you by any chance seen a naughty hobgoblin called Gobby, who is intent on turning black into white and white into black?"

"It's Madam, not Sir," growled the seal without opening her eyes. "And no, I haven't seen Gobby. Is he edible? In fact, are you edible?"

Before she could open her eyes and take a good look at him. Baby Shark rose rapidly upwards.

"She hasn't seen him," he reported briefly.

Where was Gobby? Opal banked close to a rock face where some blue-eyed shags were nesting.

"Have you seen Gobby," she called out.

"No," they replied, "we haven't seen anyone."

Next they asked some terns who were flying past, but they hadn't seen Gobby either. And when they asked some skuas, the skuas didn't even bother to reply.

"There must be some sign of him," Monkeyji said thoughtfully. "He's too mischievous not to have left a trail."

"Let's go back to Deception Island," Siril said suddenly. "If he likes living in fireplaces, he likes being warm. He'll want to get back to the steam from the volcano."

The dragons circled back, flying slowly. They saw some Orcas and humpback whales below them, but before they could even think of asking them whether they had seen Gobby, the whales had dived into the water again.

However, once they were over Deception Island they couldn't help seeing that Gobby had been at work again: an entire rock face had been turned a vivid green. Even the snow was green and some of it had melted in a green trickle. "Oh! Look at that horrible green!" Aditi cried. "And it's melting. Global warming?" she whispered to Siril. Both of them looked very sombre. Beautiful couldn't understand why they were so worried by a bit of melting ice. She would ask them later. Right now there was Gobby to deal with. He was back on his ledge, jumping forward and backward, forward and backward... and pausing every now and then to puff out his chest. He looked pleased with himself.

The dragons hovered overhead. Monkeyji descended on the seaweed rope in order to talk to Gobby. He grinned at her.

"I'm getting better, aren't I?" he said, pointing at the green rock face proudly

5

The Cold Treatment

Monkeyji regarded him with her one grey eye. "You must stop playing these silly tricks at once, young Gobby," she said severely.

"I'm not playing silly tricks," Gobby retorted. "I'm exercising my talent! And I'm improving by the minute."

"You've caused the penguins great distress, and you're vandalising the landscape," Monkeyji told him.

"I am not!" shouted Gobby indignantly. "I am using the landscape as my canvas and I am going to paint on it."

"You certainly are not," Monkeyji informed him. But as she said this, the seaweed rope broke and she fell into the icy cold water. Baby Shark and Opal dived in to look for her. Baby Shark saw her first and pushed her towards Opal. Opal seized her in one of her claws and rose into the air rapidly. She flew close to Goldie and dropped Monkeyji into the howdah as gently as she could.

On the ledge below, Gobby continued to jump forward and backward, forward and backward. He shouted up at them, "Who looks silly now? Ha!" and went on jumping.

Aditi took off Monkeyji's jacket which was dripping with water and did her best to rub her fur dry with the cloak of invisibility. Opal breathed warm air in her direction as she flew alongside Goldie. But Monkeyji's teeth were chattering and her face had turned grey.

"We must get her warm quickly," Aditi cried. "How does Gobby keep himself warm?"

"I think I know," Baby Shark exclaimed suddenly. "Take Monkeyji down to the nearest thermal vent, and huddle around her to keep her warm. I'll be back shortly." With that he shot off towards Gobby.

Goldie and Opal landed on the beach. Opal continued to blow warm air towards Monkeyji, but she had to be careful not to set the howdah on fire. The steam from the volcano helped, and Beautiful and Aditi held Monkeyji tight. But Monkeyji continued to shiver. The water had been very cold. Aditi, Beautiful, Siril and the two dragons began to worry: would Monkeyj survive? Just then Baby Shark arrived. He had his fins outspread and was balancing something carefully on his back.

"Hot water bottles!" he exclaimed. "That's Gobby's secret. He keeps a stash of them in a crevice and fills them with hot water from a thermal vent. Then he ties one in front and one on his back inside his jacket. When they get cold, he refills them."

Aditi took the hot water bottles and pressed them against Monkeyji and wrapped Monkeyji in a spare jacket. Gradually Monkeyji stopped shivering and regained her colour.

As they waited for Monkeyji to recover, they noticed that the snow above Gobby was turning an electric pink.

"Oh no," cried Aditi. "That's Gobby's work. He's doing it again!"

Goldie had had enough. "Hang on," he cried, and with the howdah still on his back and the adventurers still in it, he rose into the air and swooped down on Gobby. He hooked a talon into the back of Gobby's jacket and handed him to Opal in midair. "Set him down on that crag nearby,"

he told her. "We'll settle on the adjoining crag. When he
starts getting cold, then perhaps we'll be able to talk to him."

Opal took Gobby from Goldie and plonked him down
in the snow high on top of the crater. The two dragons
settled nearby.

"Hey!" shouted Gobby. "What do you think you're
doing?"

"Teaching you a lesson," Aditi shouted back.

"Why? I'm not doing any harm," Gobby returned.

"Yes, you are. Do you want to make the penguins
unhappy?" Aditi asked.

"No," replied Gobby.

"Do you want to make the penguins angry?" Aditi asked.

"Of course not," replied Gobby.

"Well, that's what you are doing!" shouted Beautiful.

Opal then seized Gobby again and the four adventurers, Baby Shark and the dragons flew to the Chinstrap colony.

The Chinstrap Penguins were wailing and crying and making such a noise that nobody could say anything.

Opal and Goldie looked at each other and let out a tremendous roar. The Chinstrap Penguins continued sobbing. The dragons then tried spreading their wings and making everything dark. This time it didn't work. The Chinstrap Penguins cried even more loudly.

Siril had an idea. He set to work with his magic clay and soon there were a dozen perfect Chinstrap Penguins parading in front of everyone. There  were no polka dots on them, no spots of any kind, no blotches. The Chinstrap Penguins looked at Siril's penguins in awestruck silence. Perhaps there might be hope for them?

Aditi seized her chance. "This is the goblin who is responsible for the splotches." She pushed Gobby forward. "What do you want to do with him?"

"Make him change us back to the way we were! Yes, make him change us back," they shouted in a ragged chorus. "And make sure he doesn't do it again!"

Gobby looked at the penguins. He was shocked. He hadn't thought that they would be unhappy. "I'll try," he muttered. He wasn't sure he could do it. He was too cold. His spell depended on his being able to jump back into his footsteps exactly. If he missed doing that by even a millimetre, the spell wouldn't work.

With the four adventurers and Goldie and Opal and all the penguins watching him, Gobby set to work. He jumped forward and backward, all the while shouting:

"Abracadabra.
Reverso, Converso.
Gobby was foolish and has had his fun.
He must now undo what he has done."

But though he did this over and over again, nothing happened. He was tired, and couldn't quite manage to land exactly in his footsteps when he jumped back. The Chinstrap Penguins had had their hopes raised. They were beginning to get angry. At last Opal stepped in.

"Here, we'll help," she said. "When you're jumping back, I'll catch you by the back of your jacket and keep you hovering, while Aditi sets each of your feet down in exactly the right place." They did that and after one or two tries, it worked. The Chinstrap Penguins looked like themselves again.

"Now for the Gentoo Penguins," Monkeyji said severely.

"But I'm tired," wailed Gobby.

"Too bad," retorted Aditi. Beautiful looked at her in surprise. She hadn't realised Aditi could be so severe. Gobby wasn't even allowed a place in the howdah as they flew to Cuverville Island. He dangled from a claw that Opal had hooked into the back of his jacket. They saw a hot water bottle slip out and fall into the ocean below.

"That's POLLUTION," muttered Siril.

6

It's Obvious

As soon as Aditi announced to the Gentoo Penguins on Cuverville Island, that Gobby was responsible for the zebra stripes, they got ready to lynch him. He was saved only because Beautiful stood in front of him and told him to climb on her back. He cowered there miserably, trying to make himself as small as possible. Aditi calmed down the penguins.

"Before we talk of punishment, let's at least see if he's sorry," she said to the penguins.

"Are you sorry?" she called out to Gobby.

"Y e - e - e - s ," stuttered Gobby. He was starting to shiver, both because he was afraid and because he was cold.

"Will you undo what you have done?" shouted Aditi.

"I'll try," stuttered Gobby. He slithered off Beautiful and fell on the snow. He got up and jumped forward, but when he tried to jump back he fell on his bottom.

The Gentoo Penguins started forward angrily.

"Wait," called out Opal. "Come on, Gobby," she said to the hobgoblin gently. "I'll help you. Pull yourself together."

Gobby got to his feet. Opal held him by the collar.

"Abracadabra.

Reverso, Converso.

What Gobby has done must be undone.

For the Gentoo Penguins it wasn't much fun!"

Opal helped him as he jumped back and held him in midair while Aditi place his feet carefully in his footprints. It worked. The Gentoo Penguins were their dapper selves again.

The four adventurers, Baby Shark and the dragons were getting ready to leave, when the Gentoo leader shouted, "Wait! What about his punishment?"

"He has said he's sorry. And he has removed the zebra stripes. Why not let him go?" suggested Aditi.

"No," said the leader. "He has to pay for making us miserable..."

"Well, what do you think he should do?" asked Monkeyji.

"He should give himself zebra stripes, which he has to wear for at least one day," the leader replied.

A dozen of the penguins had surrounded Gobby. He was forced to agree. He looked at Opal wearily. She helped him up by the back of his jacket and lifted him forward.

Gobby recited:

"*Abracadabra.*
Reverso, Converso.
  Gobby must do to himself
    What he did to the penguins.
    That must be so."

Aditi set his feet down carefully in his footsteps and he fell forward covered in zebra stripes.

The Gentoo Penguins were satisfied and allowed the adventurers to take him away in the howdah.

They flew back to Deception Island in cold sleet. Gobby whimpered quietly, but he didn't say a word. The adventurers felt sorry for him and left him alone. At last he spoke in a faltering voice: "Please, could you let me down near my own ledge? I'm cold and hungry and need to sleep. Tomorrow I'll go with you and do whatever you want."

It was true he was cold and hungry and needed a rest, so the adventurers let Baby Shark float him down. They were cold, hungry and tired as well. They camped where they had camped before and fell asleep. They would deal with Gobby tomorrow.

When they woke up, Opal and Baby Shark went across to fetch Gobby. He had disappeared. He had left a message for them in vivid blue lettering on the snow covered cliffside:

"Now North is South, and East is West.
You won't find Gobby though you do your best."

Opal and Baby Shark returned and reported what had happened.

"Oh no!" cried Siril. "He's reversed the North and South Poles!"

"Does that mean we're now at the North Pole?" asked Beautiful. As often happened, Beautiful was puzzled. She was used to it, but thought she had better ask.

"Yes, I suppose it does," replied Aditi.

"But then where are the polar bears and the Arctic

foxes and the narwahls and the snow owls that belong to the Arctic Circle?" she wondered. (She hadn't wanted to confuse the two poles and had checked up on the difference before they left.)

"Well, perhaps we can't see them," offered Monkeyji.

"Nothing seems to have changed very much. There's a bit more snow on the other side, but that's the only difference," protested Beautiful. "Oh look! There are some Arctic terns!"

"Yes, but they migrate to Antarctica when it's winter in the Arctic," Siril told her.

And Goldie said, "The ledge on which Gobby does his jumping is exactly where it was yesterday. The only difference is that Gobby has disappeared."

Aditi took out the compass her grandfather had given her. "The needle is pointing North just as it did yesterday," she muttered.

"On compasses the needles always do point North," Siril interjected. "I don't think that means anything."

"The thing is though, that I heard Siril say that Gobby's ledge is to the south of us. Isn't it still where it was?" wondered Beautiful. "I can see it. It's still there."

Aditi looked at the compass. "This compass says it's still South of us, but it always points to true North. Perhaps other compasses would say it's to the North of us now."

They sat there trying to work out where Gobby was, how they might find him, and which direction was which.

Suddenly Beautiful said, "I know what's happened! I know how to solve the problem!"

The others stared at her. They loved Beautiful, but they didn't think of her as a great brain.

"Well, tell us then," Siril said impatiently.

Beautiful just stood there looking smug and enjoying all the attention she was getting for a second or two. It wasn't often that she could solve a problem that had baffled the others.

"There isn't any problem," she announced grandly.

"Oh Beautiful, how can you say that?" cried Aditi. "Of course there's a problem if he's reversed the poles."

"Look around you," replied Beautiful. "Nothing has changed. He has just called 'North' 'South' and 'South' 'North.' It hasn't made any difference. It's just words. According to Gobby, we're now at the North Pole, well, sort of. But how does it matter?"

Siril looked dazed. "What about all the maps in the world? What about all the ships at sea?" he asked.

Beautiful was feeling more and more confident. "I expect they're calling 'North' 'South' 'and 'South' 'North' too and getting on just fine. It's like being in the looking glass world in which they've got their left and right the other way round. It might be 'wrong', but it works all right," she concluded triumphantly.

"Should we just leave things the way they are then?" wondered Aditi. What Beautiful had said made sense in a way, but she felt confused.

"No, no," said Beautiful. "We were used to the world the way it was. We should have it back."

"Well, then what should we do?" asked Monkeyji.

Wow! Monkeyji asking her for advice. Beautiful couldn't believe it. Why were the others having so much trouble seeing what was obvious?

"We should catch Gobby and then ask the Marine Sage what to do with him," Beautiful said nicely. She was careful not to say, "It's obvious!"

7

Gobby's Graffiti

They strapped on Goldie's howdah again, and Goldie said wearily, "Where do you think he has gone?"

"I don't think he'll go far. He likes staying near the volcano vents so that he can keep warm. Let's do a wide circle around Deception Island and see if we can find traces of him."

As they circled around, traces of Gobby were only too easy to find.

"EL REVERSO WAS HERE"

was written in large, lurid capitals on the white snow covering the rock faces. There were variations on Gobby's message:

"AND HERE."

"ALSO HERE."

"REVERSO RULES!"

"REVERSO REIGNS!"

The messages were getting more and more bumptious and the colours more varied. Though they read them all and got more and more annoyed, they couldn't find Gobby. Monkeyji was particularly distressed. "Oh, what has he done to this once unspoilt landscape!" she cried. She could hardly bear to look.

How were they to find Gobby? "I could carve some letters on that beautiful white slope over there," Baby Shark suggested. "I could write: 'GOBBY STINKS!' That would draw him out."

"It would spoil the landscape even more," Aditi pointed out. "Let's try to think of something else."

"I know!" cried Beautiful. She was feeling more and more confident after having been so clever. "Follow the Orcas!"

When the others didn't understand immediately, she explained. "Gobby needs the Orcas to get about from place to place. If we can find the Orcas, we'll find him."

"That's true," murmured Siril. "Of course, the Orcas are bad tempered and won't talk to us; but look, there are some humpbacked whales below. We could ask them."

Baby Shark was sent down to ask and soon returned with some information: they had seen a strange, small creature with a pod of Orcas in Wilhelmina Bay. The little creature was riding on the back of one of the whales.

When they got to Wilhelmina Bay, what they saw was something quite different. Gobby was perched on an ice floe. He was surrounded by Orcas. They didn't look at all friendly. It was clear why they were sometimes called killer whales. There was something odd about this particular pod. Each whale had a broad red stripe running along one side.

The whales were bumping the ice floe with their noses and making it rock dangerously. Gobby was in danger of falling into the water any moment now. Goldie flew down and scattered the Orcas with a few well chosen puffs of smoke and flame. Opal flew behind him and snatched up Gobby before the ice floe melted. She deposited him in the howdah.

The Orcas hadn't been frightened away. They were shouting something at Goldie. "Go and find out what they want," Goldie told Baby Shark.

"Don't get too close," Opal warned. "They're in a very bad temper, and might snap you up."

Baby Shark descended and hovered a safe distance from them.

"What do you want?" he shouted.

"REVENGE!" they roared. "We want him to remove this stupid red stripe he's put on us. And then we'll eat him up!"

Inside the howdah, the others glared at Gobby.

"I thought you were going to be good?" Monkeyji said.

"I was being good," Gobby retorted indignantly. "I was decorating the hillside."

"You were vandalising it!" Monkeyji snapped. The others had never heard her sound so severe.

"And what about the Orcas? They were supposed to be your friends. Why did you annoy them?" Siril asked.

"I didn't mean to annoy them. They are so streamlined and so swift, I thought I would give them a decal stripe like the kind they put on sports cars."

"They're after your blood," Aditi murmured. "Can you undo the damage?"

"Yes," muttered Gobby. "But please, I don't want to get eaten."

"I'll do my best," Goldie growled, "but I don't guarantee anything."

They found a suitable ice floe near a place where Opal could perch. Opal set down Aditi and Gobby on the floe and settled herself securely nearby. Goldie made sure the killer whales kept their distance.

Aditi, Opal and Gobby went through the jumping forward and backward routine again. This time Gobby shouted:

"Abracadabra.

Reverso, Converso.

When I cry, 'Swipe,'

Wipe that stripe!"

The red stripe along the side of the killer whales disappeared, but they were still angry. "We want Gobby! We want Gobby!" they shouted at Goldie.

While Goldie and Baby Shark tried to parley with them, Opal picked up Gobby and Aditi and deposited them in the howdah.

"We can't let him be eaten," Baby Shark explained to the Orcas. "That's too severe a punishment. Can you suggest something else?"

"Freeze him in the ice for a thousand years?" suggested one killer whale.

"Paint him red and let him stay that way forever and ever?" suggested another.

"Listen," shouted Aditi. "If we take him to the Marine Sage and let her decide what to do with him, would that be all right?"

That silenced the killer whales. They had heard of the Marine Sage. They knew who she was. All the sea creatures respected her.

"All right," the Orcas agreed. "But he must clean up first."

"Definitely," Monkeyji shouted from the howdah.

"And there's one more thing," a killer whale added, "but this is only a request: could the Marine Sage banish him from Antarctica please?"

"We'll try," replied Aditi.

"And could you tell her please that the snow is melting unusually fast. Many of us are having to move further South," the Orcas shouted.

"Yes, we will," Aditi promised.

Then they set about the tedious task of taking Gobby from rock face to rock face and making him undo the damage he had done. The lettering on the snow had melted into ugly splotches.

Aditi and Siril sighed. Even Monkeyji looked grave. "The Orcas are right. The snow does seem to be melting unusually fast," she murmured.

Beautiful couldn't understand it. "So what?" she asked. "So much the better. Perhaps we'll all feel a little warmer."

"I'll explain," Siril said. And while Opal and Aditi made Gobby undo the damage he had done, Siril tried to explain to Beautiful why the melting snow was worrying them so much.

"Look," he said to Beautiful, "all the activity on our planet has led to a rise in the long term average temperature. That's Global Warming and Climate Change."

"What's so bad about it?" asked Beautiful. "So it will be a little warmer. So what?"

"It means more extreme weather, floods, wildfires, droughts and storms. Everyone will suffer. A small rise in temperature means that the polar ice caps have started melting. If this goes on, the sea level will rise and rise and large tracts of land will go underwater. Whole cities will be destroyed and there will be death and destruction. In addition to Global Warming there's also the problem of pollution we've all caused. It accelerates Global Warming and in the oceans many species may become extinct."

Siril paused. For a few seconds Beautiful couldn't say anything. She could hardly believe her ears. What Siril was talking about was a planetwide catastrophe, vast destruction all over the earth.

"Is what you're saying true?" she asked in a small voice. It was hard to take in.

"I'm afraid so," Siril replied sadly.

"Well, we must do something! What can we do?" Beautiful cried.

"Those who understand the danger we are in are trying to do what they can to reduce pollution and the rise in temperature," Siril told her gently. "But not everyone realises how serious it all is."

Just then Aditi and Opal announced that they had finished helping Gobby clean up the mess he had made. They decided to take him to the Marine Sage so that she could deal with him. Baby Shark dived into the water briefly and set up a rendezvous with her.

8

It Was Only a Joke

Goldie and Opal were exhausted. They hadn't found enough seaweed to eat. The four adventurers and Baby Shark weren't in much better shape. They decided to rest for the night before setting off early for the small island off the west coast of South Africa where the Marine Sage had said she would meet them. They kept Gobby with them. They had buttoned him up securely in a spare jacket and tied the sleeves to a side of the howdah. With any luck that would keep him out of mischief. But in the middle of the short Antarctic night Monkeyji woke up to the sound of scuffling. Gobby had almost succeeded in wriggling out of the jacket. She roused the others. They were tired, sleepy and hungry. They glared at Gobby. What could they do with him?

Aditi had an idea. She emptied a peanut jar and gave the peanuts to Beautiful. Then she opened the Grow Small jar and rubbed the ointment on Gobby. Gobby realised what she was about to do and tried to run away, but Monkeyji caught him and popped him into the jar. Aditi closed the lid. Perhaps now they could get some sleep. They didn't get very much. In no time at all it was time to set off if they were to be on time for their appointment with the Marine Sage. Goldie rose  wearily to his feet and took off. Opal and Baby Shark followed him. In spite of being so tired they couldn't help looking at the rocky snow covered landscape and the grey sea below them. Antarctica was silent, untouched and beautiful.

Meanwhile, Gobby was banging so hard against the sides of his glass jar that he succeeded in making it fall over. Monkeyji peered at him. He looked so miserable and bedraggled that she felt sorry for him.

"Perhaps we could let him out?" she said. "Now that we're on our way he can't do much harm. And it's a long flight."

Siril and Aditi were doubtful, but agreed to let him out provided he promised to be good, which, of course, he did. Beautiful was fast asleep. Aditi let Gobby out. He sat quietly in a corner of the howdah and waited to grow back to his right size. The others fell asleep.

Beautiful woke up to find that Monkeyji was leaping about the howdah telling everyone that they had to do something. "It's urgent!" she was shouting.

"What is urgent?" asked Beautiful.

"Everything!" screeched Monkeyji. "We have to act quickly!"

Beautiful couldn't understand it. It wasn't like Monkeyji to run around like a mad thing. She appealed to Aditi. But Aditi was sitting cross-legged and appeared to be in a deep trance. She paid no attention at all when Beautiful called out to her, "Aditi! Aditi, wake up! Something is the matter with Monkeyji."

It was no use. Beautiful turned to Siril. "Siril," Beautiful cried. "Wake up, Siril. Aditi is in a trance, and Monkeyji is dashing about so wildly, she's in danger of falling out of the howdah. Oh, do wake up. We have to find out what's wrong with them and make sure they'll be all right."

"I don't want to wake up," Siril replied sleepily. "I'm having a beautiful dream."

"Oh please, Siril," Beautiful tried again. "Do be sensible. Something has gone wrong. We have to do something."

"I don't want to be sensible," Siril murmured. "That's hard work. I'd much rather dream."

That didn't sound like Siril at all. There was something wrong with him as well. It was down to her to do something. Then she saw Gobby lurking in a corner and grinning happily. Gobby! He was at the bottom of it! She seized him quickly with her trunk and held him fast. Then she called out to Baby Shark to come and help. Baby Shark couldn't believe his eyes when he saw Aditi in a trance, Siril half asleep with a silly smile on his face, and Monkeyji running about and chattering wildly.

He looked enquiringly at Beautiful.

Beautiful raised Gobby with her trunk and swung him by the heels so that he was hanging upside down. "He's at the bottom of it. He has done something to them."

By this time Gobby had stopped grinning. He was afraid Beautiful was going to throw him out of the howdah.

"P-p-please don't hurt me," he whimpered as Beautiful swung him to and fro. "I'll confess what I did. I didn't mean any harm. It was only a joke."

"WHAT DID YOU DO?" yelled Beautiful and Baby Shark together.

"Well, you see," mumbled Gobby. "I turned them into their opposites."

"I see," said Beautiful. She had already guessed that something like that had happened. "And how did you manage that?"

"My magic's getting stronger. If I concentrate hard enough, I can change things into their opposites — at least for a while," Gobby explained.

"Well, change them back again," Baby Shark told him, "or else –"

"Or else what?" asked Gobby cheekily.

"Or else I'll throw you overboard," Beautiful replied. She began swinging him slowly.

"No, no! Please don't!" Gobby shrieked. "But I can't do anything when I'm upside down. Just set me upright and I'll undo the magic."

Beautiful turned him right side up while still holding on to him and told him to get to work. Gobby concentrated hard, and after a few minutes Monkeyji settled down, Aditi came out of her trance, and Siril rubbed his eyes and became alert and wide awake. They couldn't remember properly what had happened. Beautiful and Baby Shark explained what Gobby had done.

Beautiful asked Aditi and Monkeyji to tie up Gobby securely in two of the jackets. When they had done so, she stowed him in a corner of the howdah.

"Now then, young Gobby," she said to him severely. "Stay perfectly still or else I might accidentally step on you." This so frightened Gobby that for the rest of the flight he gave no further trouble.

Beautiful turned to the others. "I don't think he'll do any more mischief. And now, I'm tired and am going to get some sleep."

"Of course you are," Monkeyji said. "It's thanks to you and Baby Shark that the three of us are now all right."

But by then Beautiful was so tired that she had fallen asleep, and Baby Shark had floated out of the howdah and rejoined Opal.

"I'm very glad Beautiful took charge and got us out of this mess, but there's one thing that puzzles me," Siril said.

"Me too," put in Monkeyji.

"I can understand why Gobby's magic didn't affect Baby Shark — he was outside the howdah. And I suppose Gobby didn't dare play tricks on Goldie. We might have all crashed. But why didn't Gobby's magic affect Beautiful? It doesn't make sense," Siril went on.

"I think I know what happened," Aditi replied. "The magic did affect Beautiful. She became everything she says she isn't, though she tries sometimes. She was calm, rational and decisive. And she was confident. She took charge and handled things beautifully."

"So then perhaps she is capable of being all that?" Monkeyji mused. "Perhaps in a way everything contains its opposite?" Then she closed her eyes and thought about it.

Aditi looked at Siril, "Do you really think I'm capable of sitting still and doing nothing when there's an emergency?"

He looked back at her. "Do you really think I'm capable of wanting to dream instead of trying to do something practical?"

"Perhaps," said Beautiful waking up briefly, "we're all capable of all sorts of things."

9

Gobby the Good

Goldie had been flying steadily meanwhile. It was almost as though he was on automatic pilot. If Baby Shark hadn't warned him, he might have overshot the tiny island where they were to meet the Marine Sage. She was waiting for them. They undid the jackets in which Gobby was tied up and Beautiful hauled him out of the howdah. She held him up by one foot and dangled him upside down when she presented him to the Marine Sage. She wasn't taking any chances.

"It's all right, Beautiful," the Marine Sage said. "You can put him down now."

Beautiful was tempted to just let go of him and let him fall to the ground, but she thought better of it. She lowered him gently so that he only felt a small bump.

Gobby stood there looking dishevelled, exhausted and very sorry for himself. He wouldn't meet the Marine Sage's eye.

"Well, Gobby, what do you have to say for yourself?" the Marine Sage asked.

"I didn't mean any harm," Gobby snivelled.

"But you did a lot of harm!" Baby Shark pointed out.

"What did he do exactly?" the Marine Sage wanted to know.

Aditi stepped forward. "He turned the rocks white and the snow black in patches. He distressed the penguins by covering them in zebra stripes and polka dots. He infuriated

the killer whales by painting a red stripe on them. He daubed the landscape of Antarctica with graffiti. And, for a while, he turned us into the opposite of ourselves."

"And he reversed the poles," Baby Shark added.

"Why did you do these things?" the Marine Sage demanded.

"Because I could," replied Gobby sullenly. Then in a fit of defiance he added, "And what's more, my magic is getting stronger and stronger. I don't need to jump back into my own footsteps any more."

"What do you think we should do with him?" The Marine Sage turned to the others.

"Well, the Orcas wanted to lynch him or freeze him in ice for a thousand years," Siril offered. "And they were his friends."

"I think the first thing to do is to deprive him of his powers," Monkeyji said mildly. "He can't be allowed to go on making everyone miserable."

The Marine Sage agreed. As she fixed him with her sea blue eyes, Gobby felt his magic drain away.

"Oh don't," he squealed. "Oh please don't. Without any magic, the other goblins will bully me more than ever."

"Serves you right!" Beautiful told him. She was very cross.

"Oh please, please, please. I'll be good from now on," Gobby cried.

"That you will," the Marine Sage said. She looked stern.

"Are you going to –" Aditi ventured to ask.

"Yes," replied the Marine Sage. "I think we'll do to him what he did to others. He's going to become the opposite of who he was. From now he'll be Gobby the Good, the kind, sweet, helpful goblin."

As she said this Gobby felt himself changing. The others, watching him, could also see a transformation. He straightened up. His expression changed. Instead of looking sly and sulky, he started to look friendly and cheerful.

Gobby couldn't understand what was happening to him. "I – I feel different," he said slowly. He looked down at himself. "Even my clothes look different. They suddenly feel fresh and clean."

The Marine Sage smiled at him. "A new Gobby, new clothes," she said.

Gobby looked at the Marine Sage uncertainly. "What happens now?" he asked. "I'm truly sorry for the things I did. I shouldn't have caused so much trouble for everyone." And he did, indeed, look remorseful.

They all began to think that he might not be a bad sort of hobgoblin after all. Monkeyji spoke up. "If we send him back to where he lived before, the other goblins will bully him mercilessly, especially now that he's a good natured hobgoblin without any powers."

"I know who might have him," Beautiful said suddenly. "Baby Shark and I both had a telepathic message from the Sibyl a few days ago saying that she was looking for someone who might help with the housework and run little errands for her. Do you think Gobby would suit? Shall I ask her?"

The Marine Sage and the adventurers thought about it. The adventurers had first met the Sybil of Cumae when they had tackled the Vesuvian Giant. She was very, very old, very, very wise and she could be cantankerous though she was not bad hearted.

"Yes, do," the Marine Sage said after a pause, and the others agreed. "The arrangement might work. Remember to tell her that Gobby has now become the opposite of who he was."

Beautiful nodded. "The Sybil knows everything anyway. But we'll explain about Gobby."

She and Baby Shark moved away from the others and concentrated hard in order to establish a telepathic link with the Sybil. She had a soft spot for them and she sometimes communicated telepathically with them. After a few minutes they came back.

"The Sybil says she'll take him on trial. In return for cleaning and sweeping and a few other tasks, he'll be given board and lodging and possibly some wages depending on how he shapes up," Beautiful reported.

"Do you think the Sybil will like me?" Gobby asked nervously. "I've heard of the Sybil. She's so old and wise that I might get on her nerves."

"She's all right really," Baby Shark reassured him "She won't hurt you. She doesn't hurt anyone."

"I'll fly you over to the Bay of Naples," Opal told Gobby, "after I've rested."

"And I'll go with you," Goldie added. "That way we can pay our respects and give her everyone's regards."

"That's settled then," the Marine Sage said.

"I have a small request," Gobby spoke diffidently. "I know I don't deserve anything from you after I've done so much mischief, but it will be lonely staying with the Sibyl. After I've done my chores I won't have anything to do except look at the blue Mediterranean, which is beautiful of course..." His voice trailed away.

"What do you want?" asked Monkeyji.

"Could I borrow your book, please?" Gobby responded.

"Do you mean the thesaurus?" Siril replied. "What will you do with it?"

"I'll look up the synonyms and antonyms and think about what is the opposite of what," Gobby answered.

"And get back to your old tricks again?" Monkeyji sounded very severe.

"Oh no!" cried Gobby. "I couldn't even if I wanted to. I'll just read about opposites and think about them."

"So that you can play some more tricks," snapped Beautiful.

"No, oh no," protested Gobby.

"Then what?" demanded Siril.

"So that I can turn bad things into good," said Gobby sweetly. "You see, now that I'm a good goblin that's what I have to do. And, who knows, perhaps someday if I'm very good or even better than good, the Sybil might teach me some magic. And then think of all the things I could do with the 'un's' and the 'de's' and the 'dis's'."

"The 'un's' and the 'de's' and the 'dis's'?" asked Baby Shark wonderingly.

"Yes!" said Gobby cheering up suddenly, "I could be unusual, uncanny, unreal, unwavering..."

"Or uncivil, unlikeable, unkind, uncaring..." Siril muttered.

Gobby was too excited to pay attention. He carried on. "Or I could deconstruct, define, decant, delineate, denote, decide... Or perhaps disinfect, disappear, disregard, dismantle, discriminate, disturb..."

"GOBBY!" they all yelled at him.

Beautiful picked him up by one leg and held him high in the air.

"Do you want to be taken the rest of the way hanging upside down?" she asked.

"No, no, no," he pleaded. "Please put me down."

Beautiful relented. And put him down.

"I was only daydreaming. I'll be good from now on. I promise," he said.

"And if you make mistakes?" asked Baby Shark.

"Well, I'll try not to," replied Gobby seriously. "I'll try to be very, very good, almost perfect."

The others couldn't help smiling at how earnest he was. Monkeyji murmured, "Can a leopard change its spots?"

"Or a mischievous goblin stay out of trouble?" Aditi added.

"Thank you for bringing him back," the Marine Sage said, "and seeing to it that he undid the damage he had done. Well, now we must concentrate on the really important work."

"And that's what you want us to get on with next?" Aditi asked.

The Marine Sage nodded. They had never seen her look so serious before. Then she smiled at them, waved goodbye and dived into the sea. Aditi and the others waved in return and headed home.

Beautiful was unusually quiet on the journey home. What had they been talking about? Aditi's grandparents were happy to see them back safe and sound. The adventurers rested and the next day Goldie and Opal took off with Gobby for the Bay of Naples in order to deliver him to the Sybil. It was only when the four adventurers were sitting together quietly that Beautiful at last blurted out what was bothering her.

"Why did the Marine Sage say she had more important things to do?" she asked the others. She sounded plaintive. "Wasn't stopping Gobby from spoiling Antarctica important?"

"Of course it was," Aditi soothed. "But even in

Antarctica, Global Warming is a far more serious problem. You see, the ice is melting."

"And it's not just a problem for Antarctica. THE WHOLE PLANET IS DANGER," Monkeyji added.

"As the temperature rises, the ice caps will melt," Siril put in. And the others added.

"The oceans will rise."

"Entire species will be wiped out."

"And there will be extreme weather. Storms and floods and wildfires and droughts will increase."

Beautiful felt very frightened. "We must stop it!" she cried. "What can we do to stop it?"

"Well, we can help," Monkeyji murmured, "but this is something everyone has to understand and do something about."

"Here are some things everyone can do," Aditi said, waving a list.

"TELL EVERYONE AND EXPLAIN HOW SERIOUS IT IS," she began.

"Waste less food," Monkeyji added.

"But I don't waste food," Beautiful protested.

"It's not just you. Everyone has to change," Aditi told her. "We have to use less water and less energy."

"And the energy we do use should be renewable — like solar power and wind power," Siril put in. "It shouldn't come from fossil fuels like coal and petroleum."

"And we have to use less plastic," Monkeyji said.

"And explain to everyone how we can all live our lives less destructively."

"YES!" agreed Beautiful enthusiastically. "Let's make fliers and distribute them."

Monkeyji demurred. "But that would use up paper. It would need to be recycled. Paper is made out of trees and we need trees."

"Well, we have to do something!" Beautiful wailed.

"We could send digital messages?" Siril suggested.

"Those would only go to people who had computers or smartphones," Aditi pointed out.

They scratched their heads and then Beautiful shouted suddenly, "I know what to do! We'll write our message on tree leaves that have fallen on the ground!"

The others stared at her.

"Well, at least the leaves would be easily compostable," Monkeyji murmured. "But how would we distribute them?"

"The wind would carry them," Beautiful said firmly.

Suddenly Siril brightened up. "Yes. We could build a windmill that would generate recyclable energy and we could use it to help us distribute our message on leaves. I will email the Techno Sage and ask if she will help us rig up something."

"Something that doesn't burn fossil fuels or use too much energy," Monkeyji warned.

"Of course," replied Siril.

In no time at all Beautiful had gathered an enormous

pile of leaves, and Aditi and Monkeyji got busy writing down the warning about Climate Change and Global Warming. Looking at all the leaves, Aditi sighed, "It's a huge task."

Monkeyji nodded. "But it has to be done," she said soberly.

Beautiful brought more and more leaves. Siril contacted the Techno Sage and started work on a design for distributing the leaves. And Aditi and Monkeyji settled down to warning the world. They all knew that there was nothing more urgent, nothing more necessary.

CUT POLLUTION
REDUCE WASTE
PLANT MORE TREES
REUSE EVERYTHING YOU CAN
SAVE ELECTRICITY

For
all the children who will be affected by
Global Warming.

The Antarctic Mission

ISBN 978-93-89203-79-0
© *text* Suniti Namjoshi
© *illustrations* Tulika Publishers
First published in India, 2020

Cover design by Roshini Pochont

Published by
Tulika Publishers, 305 Manickam Avenue, TTK Road, Alwarpet,
Chennai 600 018, India
email reachus@tulikabooks.com *website* www.tulikabooks.com

Printed and bound by
Sudarsan Graphics, Chennai, India

31901068569385